Where's Our Teacher?

To all children who have ever fearfully anticipated
a day at school with a dreaded substitute teacher

Rio Bravo-Greeley Elementary School
MISSION STATEMENT

The primary mission of Rio Bravo-Greeley School is to develop within each student
a positive self-image and to teach all students the necessary skills to enable
them to acquire and use knowledge in a positive, productive manner.

Published by Willowisp Press
801 94th Avenue North, St. Petersburg, Florida 33702

Printed in the United States of America

2 4 6 8 10 9 7 5 3 1

ISBN 0-87406-742-1

Where's Our Teacher?

**Written and illustrated by the fourth-grade students of
Susan Taylor at Rio Bravo-Greeley Elementary School, Bakersfield, California**

Bobbie Benevidez, Sara Chaffin, David Cofield, Melissa Cota, Jason Couch, Mindy Driskill, Ashley Elliott, Gina Esparza, Tommy Foust, John Gardiner, Timmy Goforth, Aaron Hughes, Layne Krause, Chris Ladd, Justine Lester, Tyler McAtee, Sayuri Morfin, Tamara Nigh, Valerie Pedraza, Tyler Phillips, Chad Popplewell, Sandra Puga, Larry Reed, Courtney Richards, Britney Riley, Alex Rodriguez, Refugio Sanchez, Daniel Smith

About *Where's Our Teacher?*

The Kids Are Authors™ Competition gave our class an opportunity to have fun creating a unique story. First, the entire class participated in choosing an unusual situation to write about. Then the students asked themselves questions like, "What could happen?" "What would you say?" and "How would you feel?"

The artwork includes self-portraits of each student in the class. One of the concerns was getting everyone to draw in approximately the same proportions. We solved this by using a penny for the students' heads and folding the drawing paper. The students drew, colored, and cut out all the pictures. These were mounted on a chalk background, which was selected just for fun.

One day the boys and girls in our class were lined up waiting to see who their substitute would be.

"I hope it's not that mean lady again," said Aaron.

Ashley yelled, "Get straight so she'll think we're the best."

Just then Tyler shouted, "Whoa, look at that cowboy!"

The cowboy came straight to our class, walked in, and said, "Howdy, partners! My name is Doug, and we're going to have a boot-scootin' boogie day."

All mouths dropped open, and it was so quiet you could hear the whistle from a swinging rope.

It was time for vocabulary. Quick as a draw Cowboy Doug began writing.

John's hand shot up, and before he was called on he exclaimed, "I'm confused."

Doug explained, "These are brands and names of ranches. We have the W Diamond M, Circle L, Lazy E, Bar B, and Rocking J."

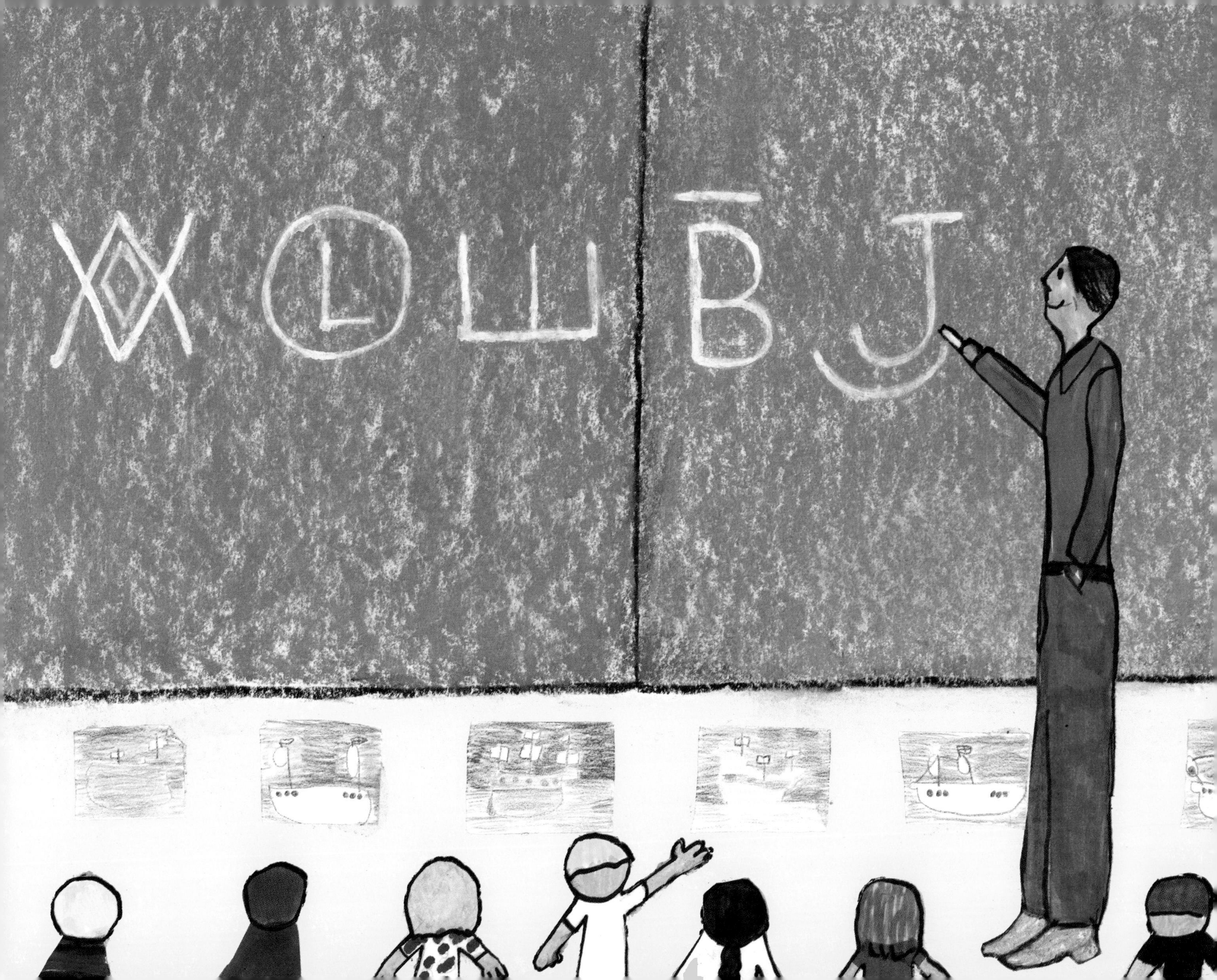

For reading, Doug handed out cowboy stories. We read about a cowboy who slept with one eye open while on a cattle drive. This was important so rustlers or wild animals wouldn't get to the cows.

We pushed back our desks for math and were divided into sets. Some students were cowfolks. The others were cows.

The cows were rounded up, moved in and out of the herd, and team penned. They were very happy when Cowboy Doug called, "Time for grub!"

While we were lining up for lunch, Cowboy Doug announced, "Today we are going to eat real cowboy food."

"What's that?" asked Chad.

"Why, it's beans and beef jerky," Doug said.

"Oh no!" Bobbie cried.

Mindy and Sara stuck out their tongues and said, "Blah!"

That afternoon during social studies, we learned about the taming of the West. Cowboy Doug showed us pictures of a wagon train. He explained how danger lurked behind every corner and behind every tree. Sometimes the people ran out of food and didn't even have beans and beef jerky.

Last of all we went out for P.E. We learned how to lasso.

"Cool," murmured Jason.

Just before class was over, our principal, Mr. Unruh, came out to ask if Cowboy Doug could come back the next day.

"Sorry," said Doug, "tomorrow I have to be home on the range."

The next day, everyone thought that things would return to normal.

Then the door opened and in walked
. . . **AN INDIAN!**

Kids Are Authors™
C O M P E T I T I O N
Books written by children for children

··

School Book Fairs, Inc., established the Kids Are Authors™ Competition in 1986 to encourage children to read and to become involved in the creative process of writing. Since then, thousands of children have written and illustrated picture books as participants in the Kids Are Authors™ Competition.

The winning books in the annual competition are published by Willowisp Press® and distributed in the United States and Canada.

For the official rules on the
Kids Are Authors™ Competition, write to:

<table>
<tr><td>In the U.S.A.,</td><td>In Canada,</td></tr>
<tr><td>Trumpet Book Fairs</td><td>Trumpet Book Fairs</td></tr>
<tr><td>Kids Are Authors™ Competition</td><td>Kids Are Authors™ Competition</td></tr>
<tr><td>801 94th Avenue North</td><td>257 Finchdene Square, Unit 7</td></tr>
<tr><td>St. Petersburg, Florida 33702</td><td>Scarborough, Ontario M1X 1B9</td></tr>
</table>

Published winners in the annual Kids Are Authors™ Competition

1994: **Where's Our Teacher?** (U.S. winner) by fourth graders of Rio Bravo-Greeley Elementary School, Bakersfield, California.
How Eagle Got His Good Eyes (Canadian winner) by fifth and seventh graders of Oscar Blackburn School, South Indian Lake, Manitoba.
Lunch with Alex (Honor Book) by first graders of Hollis Hand Elementary School, La Grange, Georgia.

1993: **A Day in the Desert** (U.S. winner) by first graders of Robert Taylor Elementary School, Henderson, Nevada.
The Shoe Monster (Canadian winner) by first and second graders of North Shuswap Elementary School, Celista, British Columbia.

1992: **How the Sun Was Born** (U.S. winner) by third graders of Drexel Elementary School, Tucson, Arizona.
The Stars' Trip to Earth (Canadian winner) by eighth graders of Ecole Viscount Alexander, Winnipeg, Manitoba.

1991: **My Principal Lives <u>Next</u> <u>Door!</u>** by third graders of Sanibel Elementary School, Sanibel, Florida.
I Need a Hug! (Honor Book) by first graders of Clara Barton Elementary School, Bordentown, New Jersey.

1990: **There's a Cricket in the Library** by fifth graders of McKee Elementary School, Oakdale, Pennsylvania.

1989: **The Farmer's Huge Carrot** by kindergartners of Henry O. Tanner Kindergarten School, West Columbia, Texas.

1988: **Friendship for Three** by fourth graders of Samuel S. Nixon Elementary School, Carnegie, Pennsylvania.

1987: **A Caterpillar's Wish** by first graders of Alexander R. Shepherd School, Washington, D.C.

1986: **Looking for a Rainbow** by kindergartners of Paul Mort Elementary School, Tampa, Florida.

To order Kids Are Authors™ titles, call Willowisp Press® at **1-800-877-8090**. In Canada, call **1-800-387-5360**.